Giddy Up, Cowgirl

★ JARRETT J. KROSOCZKA ★

VIKING

VIKING
Published by Penguin Group
Penguin Young Readers Group, 345 Hudson Street, New York, New York 10014, U.S.A.

Penguin Books Ltd, Registered Offices: 80 Strand, London WC2R 0RL, England

First published in 2006 by Viking, a division of Penguin Young Readers Group

10 9 8 7 6 5 4 3 2 1

Book design by Jim Hoover Set in Grumble and Frank Dirty
Manufactured in China

LIBRARY OF CONGRESS CATALOGING-IN-PUBLICATION DATA
Krosoczka, Jarrett.
Giddy up, Cowgirl / by Jarrett J. Krosoczka.
p. cm.
Summary: While running errands with her mother, a young girl who likes to dress
as a cowgirl tries to be helpful but her efforts always seem to backfire.
ISBN 0-670-06050-X (hardcover)

[1. Helpfulness—Fiction. 2. Mothers and daughters—Fiction.]
I. Title.
PZ7.K935Gid 2006
[E]—dc22
2005017740

For Ashley, Allison,
and Amanda

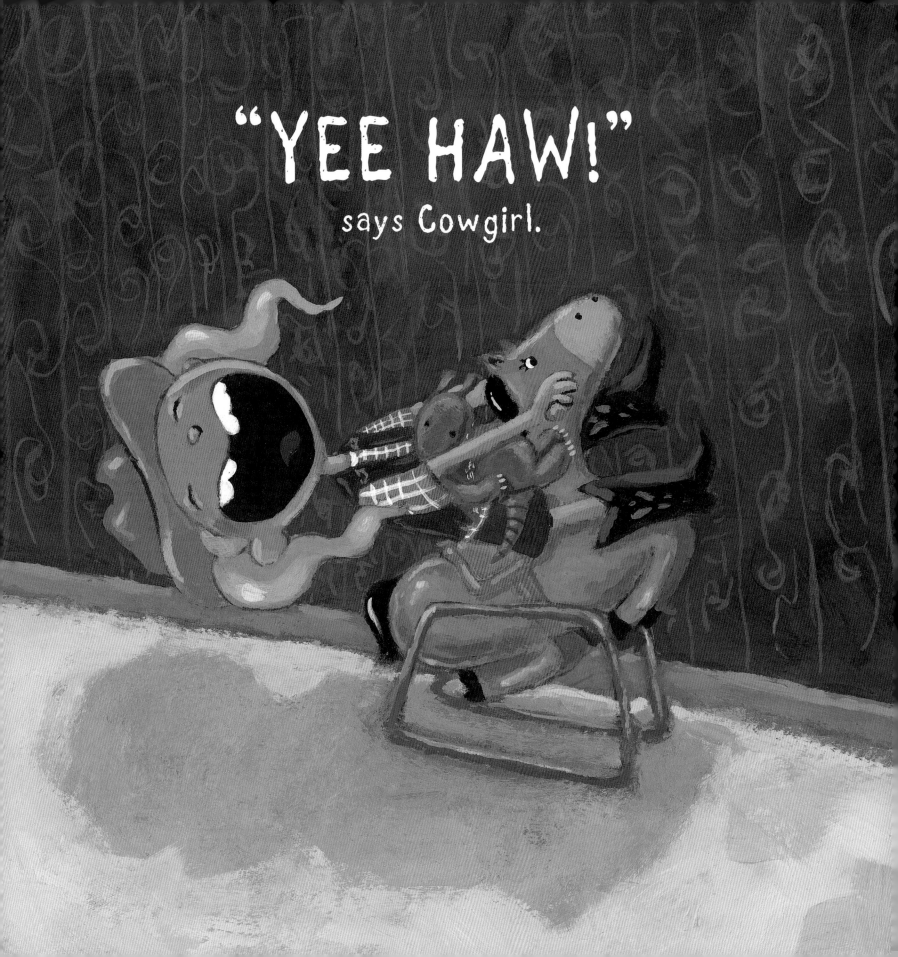

"Now remember, Cowgirl, I need you to be helpful," says Momma.

"Saddle up, Ol' Jim!"
Cowgirls *LOVE* to be helpful.

Momma can't find her checkbook.
"I'll help you find it, Momma."
Cowgirls love to find things.

"'Scuse me, pardner."

Cowgirls are good at mailing letters . . .

. . . and they are also very strong.

"I'll hold the grocery list," says Cowgirl.

"You're so helpful," says Momma.

"Jumping jeepers! It's windy!" exclaims Cowgirl.

"Don't worry,
Momma. I remember
EVERYTHING
on that list."

"Chocolate, jellybeans, marshmallows, ice cream, popsicles, cupcakes ..."

Momma is losing her patience.

"Tarnation!" cries Cowgirl.
"The bag ripped!"

"I'm sorry, Momma.
I was trying to help you."

"Accidents can happen, Cowgirl.
Just remember, your momma loves you . . ."

"... because you always try. Now let's go home and make some marshmallow sandwiches!"